The boys and girls rode
on the bus with their
teacher, Miss Royal.
The class was on a field
trip to the aquarium.

1

When the bus arrived at the aquarium, Miss Royal said, "Please choose a partner and a helper mom or dad."

"Look for the animal
you picked to study,"
Miss Royal said. "Join
me back here in an hour."

Troy and Joyce looked at the poison dart frog. "I love to play darts," Joyce said, "but I have never played darts with a frog!"

Moya and Conroy went
to study their choice,
the octopus.

"I wish I had eight arms
to clean my room!"
Conroy said.

"Can I see the octopus
squirt a cloud of ink to
hide from its enemies?"
Moya asked.

"Not here in the aquarium," said Miss Royal, "but it can squirt ink in the sea."

Ramon and Mollie found
their animal, the seahorse.
"I have never seen a horse
in the sea," Mollie said.

A helper dad added,
in a low voice, "This
small animal can eat
3,000 shrimp in a day!"

Kai-Ying and Marge
found their oyster farm.
"This makes me hungry,"
Kai-Ying said. "I enjoy
oysters cooked in oil."

Floyd and Roy found
the guitarfish.
Roy asked with a smile,
"Can he sing, too?"

12

Soon it was time for
the trip back to school.
"Elroy and I chose the
pajama fish," said Sandy
to Kai-Ying. "I like it. It is
shy like me."

Back in the classroom, each team made drawings and wrote stories about their animal.

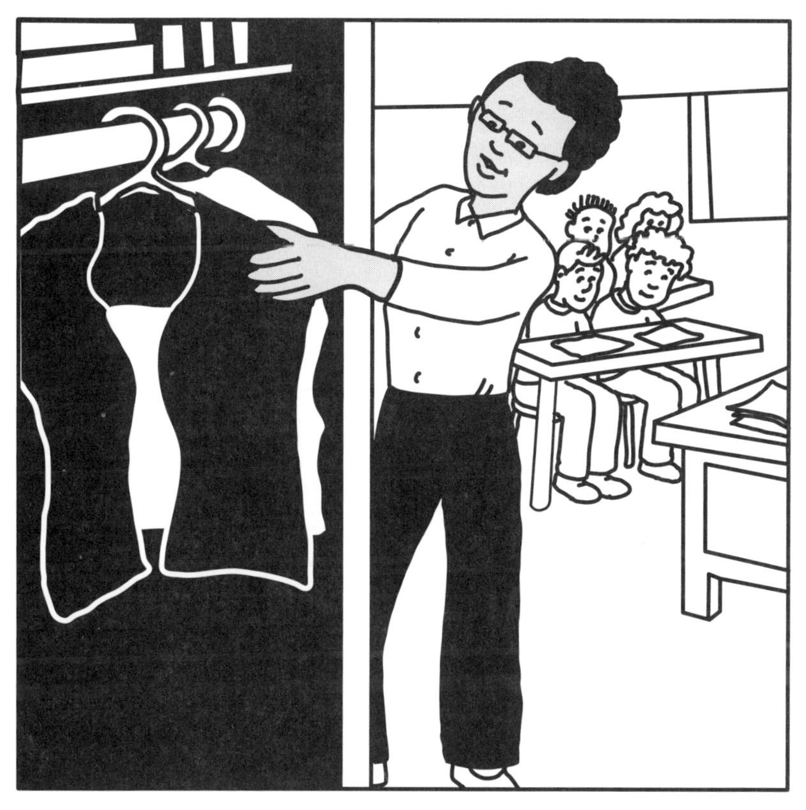

Now it was time for
Miss Royal to share the
animal of her choice.
She reached for her
black shawl.

She said, "The animal that I like the best is the royal penguin!"